The BiG Book of Dragons

If you enjoy The Big Book of Dragons,
then you'll love these three huge collections
of fantastic stories:

The Big Magic Animal Book
The Marmalade Pony *by Linda Newbery*
Mr Wellington Boots *by Ann Ruffell*
The Wishing Horse *by Malcolm Yorke*

The Big Haunted House Book
Bumps in the Night *by Frank Rodgers*
Spooky Movie *by Claire Ronan*
Scarem's House *by Malcolm Yorke*

The Big Wicked Witch Book
Fisherwitch *by Susan Gates*
Broomstick Services *by Ann Jungman*
The Cleaning Witch *by Cecilia Lenagh*

The Big Book of Dragons

School For Dragons
ANN JUNGMAN

The Bad-Tempered Dragon
JOAN LENNON

The Little Pet Dragon
PHILIPPA GREGORY

Hippo

Scholastic Children's Books,
Commonwealth House, 1–19 New Oxford Street,
London, WC1A 1NU, UK
a division of Scholastic Ltd
London ~ New York ~ Toronto ~ Sydney ~ Auckland

Published in this edition by Scholastic Ltd, 1998

The Little Pet Dragon
First published in the UK by Scholastic Ltd, 1994
Text copyright © Philippa Gregory, 1994
Illustrations copyright © David Wyatt, 1994

School for Dragons
First published in the UK by Scholastic Ltd, 1997
Text copyright © Ann Jungman, 1997
Illustrations copyright © John Eastwood, 1997

The Bad-Tempered Dragon
First published in the UK by Scholastic Ltd, 1998
Text copyright © Joan Lennon, 1998
Illustrations copyright © Serena Feneziani, 1998

Cover illustration copyright © Valeria Petrone, 1998

ISBN 0 590 54358 X

Typeset by M Rules
Printed by Richard Clays Ltd, Suffolk

2 4 6 8 10 9 7 5 3 1

The rights of the authors and illustrators to be identified
respectively as author and illustrator of their work have
been asserted by them in accordance with the
Copyright, Designs and Patents Act, 1988.

Contents

School for Dragons

ANNE JUNGMAN

Illustrated by John Eastwood

To Darcy with love

Chapter 1

The Fire

Class 4J were spending the last twenty minutes of Thursday afternoon the way they spent the last twenty minutes of every afternoon. Mrs Jeffries was reading to them. No one could read a book like Mrs Jeffries – she had a different voice for every character and whenever there was a bit of suspense her voice went quiet and you could hear a pin drop.

On the particular Thursday afternoon when our story begins, Mrs Jeffries was reading her class *The Lion, the Witch and*

the Wardrobe and they had just got to the part where Aslan is tied down on the Stone Table. The children were staring at Mrs Jeffries, their eyes bright with interest and some with a tear beginning to well up, as they thought of the noble lion in the power of the White Witch. Then the firebell went.

"Oh, no!" groaned the children. "Do we have to go?"

"Yes, of course you do," said Mrs Jeffries briskly, grabbing the register with one hand and her whistle with the other. "Now quickly line up at the door as fast as you can. Darren, just *leave* everything and line up. Right, now, out into the playground through the hall door."

"What a dozy time to have a fire drill," moaned Lisa. "Just when the story was getting really interesting."

"I know," agreed Jessie. "I mean, I've seen the story on television and I know what's going to happen, but I was really enjoying it anyway."

"What does happen?" asked Nelson eagerly. "I've never seen the TV version. Does the wicked witch really kill Aslan?"

By then they were out in the playground and lining up with the rest of the school. Mrs Jeffries blew her whistle and then started to take the register in an irritated way.

"She thinks it's a silly time to have a fire drill too," Lisa whispered to Jessie, who nodded vigorously.

Suddenly someone called out: "Look! Look at the stockroom – there really *is* a fire!"

The whole school turned and looked at the hut near the kitchen, and there, sure enough, smoke was pouring out of the window. Inside they could see a few red and purple flames.

Just then the sounds of three fire engines could be heard, swooping down on the school. Mr Wilkinson, the headteacher, stood in front of all the children.

"All right everyone, that was great. You all walked out very sensibly. I'm proud of you. We don't think the fire is in any danger of spreading to the school but better safe than sorry. Now is everyone's register complete?" he asked the teachers. "No one's been burned to a cinder?"

All the children laughed as the teachers told the head that everyone was present and correct.

"Right," said Mr Wilkinson. "I want everyone to stand up against the far fence to make way for the fire engines. Off you go now, quickly!"

Once the children were all safely out of the way, the fire engines sailed into the playground, alarm lights flashing and bells ringing. The firemen leapt down and within seconds were spraying the stockroom with great blasts of water.

One of the firemen went up to Mr Wilkinson. "Any idea what might have started the fire, sir?"

"None at all – it's a complete mystery. In fact, now I come to think of it, no one has asked me for the key to the stockroom today. No, I just can't imagine how this happened."

It only took the fire brigade five minutes to put the fire out, and all the children cheered as the firemen took a bow. One of the firemen climbed in through the broken window and then shouted out in a loud voice, "He's in here, I've got the culprit. Stand back everyone, I'm bringing him out!"

The whole school strained to see the criminal who had started the fire.

"It must be a tramp who lit a cigarette," whispered Lisa.

"Or one of those people who start fires all the time."

"An arsonist," contributed Nelson.

"Yes, that's what I meant, one of them."

But when the fireman came out he was holding a small creature in his

arms. The creature had his head buried
in the fireman's shoulder.

"It's a dragon!" said the fireman in an
amazed tone. "It's a little dragon, and he
started the fire!"

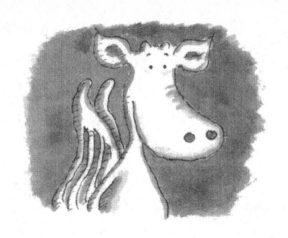

Chapter 2

M1

The whole school stared at the fireman and the bundle in his arms with utter amazement. Mr Wilkinson was the first one to find his tongue.

"All right everyone, now the fire's over and we know what caused it, we can all relax. I bet none of you thought it was a dragon – I certainly didn't. You all behaved very sensibly in the crisis; well done. It's about two minutes to home time, so will you get into lines in front of your teachers? Good. Now lead on, back into your classrooms, get your bags and coats and by then the bell should have gone."

"What do you think is going to happen to the dragon?" whispered Jessie, as they got into line again.

"The police will come and take him away, I suppose," answered Lisa.

"We don't know anything about it," Nelson pointed out. "We don't even know if it *is* a he. It might be a lady dragon."

"Whichever sex it is, it must be a baby dragon," commented Lisa. "I mean, it was so little the fireman could carry it out."

"All right, children, lead on," said Mrs Jeffries, and they began to walk back to the classroom.

"I'm not going home until I know what happened to that little dragon," said Jessie.

"Me neither," agreed Lisa.

"Are you two going to play after school?" asked Nelson.

"Yes," the two girls told him.

At that moment the bell rang.

"Put your chairs on the tables please," Mrs Jeffries told them. "Now off you go and let's hope that tomorrow isn't quite such an exciting day. Good afternoon, everyone."

"Good afternoon, Mrs Jeffries; good afternoon, everyone," chorused the children and they ran out talking about the fire and the dragon.

Lisa, Jessie and Nelson hung back. "Please, Mrs Jeffries, can we tidy up the classroom?"

Their teacher smiled at them. "Just dying to know about the dragon, aren't you?"

"Yes, Mrs Jeffries," they confessed.

"Well, why don't you pick everything up off the floor, make sure all the books are in tidy piles and that all the pencils are sharpened? Then come to the staffroom and I'll tell you what's happening with the dragon."

So the three children raced around the classroom, picking up every bit of rubbish on the floor and chucking it in the rubbish bin. Then Lisa stacked the books tidily, while Nelson tidied the book corner and Jessie sharpened the pencils.

"We've finished!" shouted Nelson. "Come on, let's go and tell Mrs Jeffries."

The three children raced as fast as they could down the stairs, through the hall and along the corridor. They stood outside the staffroom door and heard a lot of talk, and someone crying loudly.

"You knock," whispered Nelson.

"No, you," said Lisa.

"I'll do it," interrupted Jessie, and she knocked twice.

Mr Wilkinson opened the door. Looking past him the three children saw the dragon sitting on Mrs Jeffries' knee, weeping miserably.

"I didn't mean to start a fire," sobbed the dragon. "Really I didn't."

"Then what were you doing in the stockroom?" asked Mrs Jeffries gently.

The dragon gulped a few times, then blew his nose on Mrs Jeffries' hankie and said, "I wanted to look at the picture books."

There was a stunned silence.

"But you could do that at a library, couldn't you?" asked Mr Wilkinson.

"No, I couldn't," wept the dragon. "They don't want dragons in libraries, they're frightened we'll start a fire. So there isn't anywhere for me to look at books."

At that moment Mr Wilkinson remembered that Jessie, Nelson and Lisa were there. "What can I do for you three?" he asked.

"We wanted to tell Mrs Jeffries that we've finished tidying up the classroom."

"All right, very good," said the head. "I'm sure she heard you, so you can go off home now."

"No!" cried Mrs Jeffries. "These are

three of my best readers and I think they may be able to help us."

So the three children went into the staffroom and looked curiously at the little dragon. They decided it looked very small and sad, and not at all frightening.

"So you like looking at books, do you?" Mrs Jeffries asked the dragon.

"Oh, yes," replied the dragon, cheering up a bit. "I really do, better than anything."

"And can you read?"

"Oh, no," said the dragon, shaking his head sadly. "My dad says that dragons don't need to know how to read or learn any of the things that go on in a school, but I would so love to learn." And another tear ran down his nose.

Mrs Jeffries gave the dragon a hug, and kissed the top of his head. "Now here are my friends Nelson, Jessie and Lisa – they're all in my class and they are good readers. Maybe, if you ask nicely, they'd be willing to read to you."

"Oh, yes!" cried all three children at once.

"I'd love to," added Lisa.

"So would I," agreed Jessie.

"Cool!" said Nelson.

"But you'd have to promise not to burn us or anything," said Lisa.

"Oh, I wouldn't," said the dragon. "I only started the fire in the stockroom because I got so excited about the pictures in the book that I forgot."

"Do you think you can manage not to get too excited?" asked Mrs Jeffries.

"Oh, yes," the dragon assured her. "If I keep saying to myself 'no flames, no flames' it's all right, nothing but a bit of smoke now and again."

"Then we would love to read to you," agreed the children.

"Well, now that we've settled things, what are we going to do about getting you home, young man – I mean, young dragon?" demanded Mr Wilkinson.

"I can find my own way back, sir," said the dragon.

"Good," said Mr Wilkinson. "But I want your word that you won't creep into the stockroom again to read and start another fire."

"Oh, I won't, I promise I won't," said the dragon, shaking his head. "Oh, no, I'll never do that again. And thank you for not calling the police, my dad would have been very angry. May I go now?"

"Of course," said Mr Wilkinson. "And there are a few old books here that we were going to throw away. Would you like them?"

"Books for me?" The dragon's eyes lit up. "Books that I can take home for my very own? Oh, thank you, thank you. You are very, very kind. Oh, thank you," and he grabbed the books.

"We'll take you as far as the school gates," said Nelson.

"Yes," agreed Lisa. "And then we can make a date to read to you."

As they walked towards the gate the dragon began to look through his books. "They look very good. I can't wait to get them home."

"Would you like to know what they're called?" asked Lisa.

"We could tell you all that kind of thing," added Nelson eagerly.

"Do you have a name?" asked Lisa.

"It feels a bit odd calling you 'little dragon'. Do dragons have names?"

"Oh, yes," the little dragon assured them. "They most certainly do. My name is M1."

"M1!" cried the children in disbelief. "But that's the name of a road."

"Is it?" said the dragon. "Well, it's my name too. I'm the eldest boy child, you see. M for male, 1 for eldest."

"So what are your sisters called?" enquired Jessie.

"Well, there's F1, F2 and F3. F for female. My brothers are called M2 and M3."

"Oh," said the children, a bit stumped for words.

"Well, I'll take the books and be gone then," smiled the dragon.

"No, don't go till we've made an arrangement to read to you," cried Nelson.

"It'll have to be after school," chimed in Jessie.

"Be here at four o'clock tomorrow," said Lisa. "By that time all the other children will have gone. We'll talk to Mrs Jeffries tomorrow about where to go. She'll help."

"Yes," agreed Nelson. "She always knows what to do."

The dragon beamed at them and said, "See you tomorrow then."

"See you tomorrow," the children called after him. "Bye, M1."

Chapter 3

Reading

The next day the three children could hardly wait for four o'clock.

"Do you think M1 will really turn up?" asked Lisa.

"Of course he will," retorted Nelson. "I mean, he's dead keen to know what's in all those books Mr Wilkinson gave him."

At break time Mrs Jeffries was on playground duty. The three children went up to her.

"Please miss, M1 wants us to read him some stories."

"Yes, and we arranged to meet M1 here at school, at four o'clock this afternoon."

"And we told M1 that you would let us go somewhere quiet to do it," concluded Jessie.

"Now just a minute, you three," said Mrs Jeffries. "What's all this about the M1 motorway?"

"Not the M1 motorway, miss. M1, the little dragon who started the fire."

"What an odd name," said Mrs Jeffries, frowning.

"It's because he's the first male child,"

Nelson told her. "M is for male and 1 is for first. His brothers are called M2 and M3."

"Yes, and his sisters are called F1, F2 and F3," added Lisa.

Mrs Jeffries laughed. "Oh, well, at least dragons don't have any arguments about what to call their children."

"But Miss, *can* we read to him?" asked Nelson anxiously. "We did promise and he seemed really enthusiastic."

"You've twisted my arm. All right, bring him to the classroom, and I'll stay late and tidy up while you lot read to him."

That afternoon, as soon as school finished, the children went and hovered around the school gate, waiting for the dragon. At ten past four he still wasn't there.

"He's not coming," said Jessie sadly.

"It's really odd because he was dying to hear the stories," frowned Lisa.

"Look!" cried Nelson. "Look behind that tree over there."

All three children looked, and sure enough there was a small puff of smoke rising up into the air. All three ran over to the tree and there stood the dragon, carrying all the books he'd been given the previous day.

"Hello, M1, said Nelson. "We've been waiting for you."

"What are you doing behind the tree?" asked Jessie.

"I didn't dare go into the school," whispered the dragon. "My dad says that I shouldn't have gone into the school yesterday and that schools are for children and not dragons and that the teachers wouldn't let me in after the fire. So I wasn't sure that you meant what you said yesterday."

"Of course we did," said Nelson.

"Yes, and Mrs Jeffries is staying late, so that we can read to you in the classroom," added Lisa.

The dragon grinned from ear to ear.

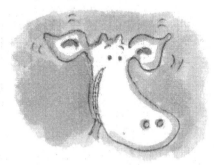

"Oh, thank you," he said. "Thank you very, very much."

So the four of them went into the classroom and the children took it in turns to read to the dragon. M1 listened intently to every word, laughing loudly at all the jokes, and biting his paws during the exciting bits. By 5.30 the children had read him three stories each.

"Time to go home, you four," said Mrs Jeffries.

"Just one more story, oh, please, please," begged M1.

"Well, all right," agreed the teacher. "But this definitely has to be the last one."

Every day on the dot of four o'clock M1 turned up to be read to. But now the summer holidays were coming and neither Mrs Jeffries nor the children were sure what to do.

"I think M1 should learn to read," declared Mrs Jeffries. "I mean, we can't always be here to read to him. I think M1 should come to school."

"What, *this* school?" asked the three children in amazement.

"And why not?" replied their teacher. "He's just as keen to learn as any of you."

So that afternoon when M1 turned up, the children asked him if he'd like to come to school and learn to read. The little dragon's eyes shone for a moment and then filled with tears. "Oh, I'd love to, it would be a dream come true; but my dad would never let me. My dad doesn't believe in education for dragons."

"Would you ask your dad to come and see me, M1? Then I'll see if I can persuade him to let you come to school," said Mrs Jeffries.

"I'll try," agreed the little dragon. "But I don't think he'll listen. He has very strong views, my dad, he really does."

The next day a very big, fierce-looking
dragon turned up with M1.

"My boy here says you want to see me," boomed Mr Dragon. "Some nonsense about teaching him to read. I hope he hasn't been bothering you or getting up to any mischief. You just tell me if he's out of order and I'll soon sort him out."

M1 stood by his father looking very worried.

"Oh, no, on the contrary, he has been coming to school every afternoon so that we can read him stories."

"Stories!" exclaimed Mr Dragon. "Waste of time, stories, if you ask me. Stories never did anyone any good. We don't have stories in our house, and a good thing too."

"Oh, I don't agree!" said Mrs Jeffries firmly. "Stories are the spice of life. Now, what I wanted to say to you was that M1 seems very keen to learn to read and I would love to teach him. If I could persuade the headteacher to take him on, would you let M1 come to school?"

"School?" shouted Mr Dragon. "*School!* Whoever heard of a dragon going to school? No child of mine is going to get mixed up with all this education lark, and that's that."

M1 looked very miserable. Nelson looked at him and thought fast. "That's a

shame," he said. "Because every night I read to my brothers and sisters. My mum always says she doesn't know how she'd cope if I wasn't there to read them all a goodnight story. I've got five younger brothers and sisters just like M1. If M1 could read he'd be no end of a help to Mrs Dragon."

M1 grinned at Nelson. "It would be great, Dad. You know how cross you get when you get home from work and all the little ones are making a noise and rampaging. I could take them all upstairs and read to them."

"Yes," agreed Jessie. "And you could eat your dinner in peace and quiet."

"And you could sit by the fire and have a nice peaceful smoke of your pipe," added Lisa.

"I don't smoke a pipe," grumbled Mr Dragon. "Dragons don't need to. Still, it would be nice to come home to a quiet house."

"And you and Mrs Dragon could discuss what you've been doing during the day," added Mrs Jeffries. "And have a peaceful cup of tea together."

"Oh, do say 'yes', Mr Dragon," begged Lisa. "We all like M1 so much."

"Please, Dad," added M1 nervously. "I would really love to be able to read."

"Oh, I suppose so," groaned Mr Dragon. "I'm beginning to see that this reading lark has a good side to it. You can go to school, son, for one term, and then I'll have to review the situation. You'll be the first dragon ever to go to school; we'll have to see how it goes.

What your grandfathers would say I hate to think. They'll be turning in their graves I shouldn't wonder."

M1 jumped up and down with delight and then gave his father a big hug.

"I'll talk to Mr Wilkinson tomorrow," said Mrs Jeffries. "And hopefully, at the beginning of next term our very first dragon pupil will join the school."

Chapter 4

Problems

Of course Mr Wilkinson did agree to let M1 join the school. "Any young creature who is as keen to learn as M1 is very welcome in my school," he declared. "So, M1, I expect to see you on the first day of next term and I hope your enthusiasm proves to be infectious."

On the first day of the new term M1 turned up in uniform – blue jeans and a T-shirt with the "Merringham Juniors" logo on it. Lisa, Nelson and Jessie ran over to him.

"You just stick with us," they told him. "You'll soon get the hang of it."

Some of the children ran up to them, calling, "Isn't that the dragon that started the fire in the stockroom?"

M1 looked upset. "I didn't mean to, really I didn't," he told them.

At that moment the whistle blew and the children went into the hall for assembly.

Mr Wilkinson welcomed them all back and made a few jokes. Then he told the school that they had a new pupil, a pupil with a difference. "Stand up M1, and come up here beside me," he said.

Treading gingerly, M1 made his way through the children to the headteacher.

"Now, children, this is M1. Most of you will remember M1 from the

time he accidentally set fire to the stockroom. M1, I want you to tell all the children here just why you did that."

M1 looked at his feet. "I wanted to look at all the pictures in the books."

"And now tell the children why it is you want to come to school."

M1 managed a small smile.

"Because I want to learn to read, more than anything in the whole wide world."

A murmur of surprise went through the hall.

"So put your hands up everyone who is going to help M1," said Mr Wilkinson.

Every hand in the hall shot up. M1 beamed at them all.

"Good," said the headteacher. "Now, M1, I want you to tell us all about yourself and your family, and why you're called M1, and why you're not dangerous."

So, blushing and shifting from one leg to the other, M1 told the children about his family.

"There are eight in my family – six children and my mum and dad, Mr and Mrs Dragon. I am called M1 because I am the first son – M for male and 1 for first. My mum and dad don't believe in education for dragons so I am the very first dragon in the whole world to ever come to a school."

Mrs Williams, the deputy head, put her hand up. "M1, I confess that I am a bit worried in case there's another fire.

I wonder if you could put my mind at rest on this matter."

M1 looked tearful. "I only blow flames when I get excited," he whispered. "And I am going to try never to let excitement get the better of me."

"And just in case M1 *does* get excited," added Mr Wilkinson quickly, "I have installed two fire extinguishers in every room in the school, including the stockroom, just in case of an unexpected emergency. So I don't think we have anything to worry about. Isn't that right, M1?"

The dragon nodded vigorously.

"Now I want you all to be very welcoming and helpful to our first dragon pupil and enjoy being different from every other school in the world."

Back in the classroom, M1 sat at the same table as Lisa, Nelson and Jessie. They promised Mrs Jeffries and the other children that if ever M1 did get excited they would grab the nearest fire

extinguisher. On the first day M1 put on an apron and began to paint a picture, something he had never done before. M1 loved covering the paper with brightly-coloured paint. When he had finished he stood back and looked at his work.

"Isn't it wonderful?" he exclaimed, jumping up and down. "Just look at that – my first painting in the whole world. I can't wait to show it to my mum and dad and M2 and M3 and F1, F2 and F3."

A little flame darted out of his left nostril.

"Fire!" yelled Lisa and all the children picked up their jars and doused M1 with the dirty-coloured water.

M1 looked completely bewildered and then giggled. "I got excited, didn't I?"

"You certainly did," agreed Mrs Jeffries. "Now come on, M1, we'll go to the staffroom and find you a spare school uniform. You must take yours home to be washed."

After that everything went smoothly. M1 learned to read incredibly fast and after a few weeks he had almost caught up with Lisa, Jessie and Nelson. Every day M1 got a gold star for reading and went home with at least two books in his rucksack. When he wasn't playing with his friends, he would sit in the book corner buried in a book.

"If only all our children were like M1," sighed Mr Wilkinson. "Hard working, enthusiastic, helpful and polite. Maybe I should open a school for dragons."

There were a few more little fiery problems. One day in the playground M1 was skipping with some of the girls and having lots of fun turning the rope and singing:

"Jelly on a plate,
Jelly on a plate,
Wibble wobble, wibble wobble,
Jelly on a plate."

Unfortunately, as the pace quickened and the girls ran into the rope faster and faster, M1 started laughing and blowing fire. The rope caught alight.

In a flash the teacher on duty rushed across and threw her coat over the flames and M1, and rolled over on top of them. In a few moments the fire was out and M1 peeped out of the teacher's coat, coughing and gasping.

"Sorry, M1," said the teacher. "I hope I didn't crush you, but I had to put the flames out."

"I'm all right," wheezed M1. "I don't know what happened."

"You must have got excited," the teacher told him.

"Sorry," mumbled M1. "I didn't mean to."

After that there were hardly any more fires and M1 began to win every prize in the school for good work.

"Well," said Mr Wilkinson at a staff meeting. "We seem to have absorbed young M1 painlessly into our school; I don't see any problems ahead."

But Mr Wilkinson was wrong. For the very next day he got a letter saying that an inspector was coming into the school to look at the children's written work and use of language.

"An inspector," groaned the headteacher to Mrs Jeffries. "Just as everything was going so nicely.

"Let any number of inspectors come!" declared Mrs Jeffries. "This is an excellent school, and we've got nothing to hide."

"I don't know about that," sighed Mr Wilkinson. "We've got M1 to hide for a kick-off!"

Chapter 5

The Inspector

On the day of the inspection the children all sat in neat rows in the hall, waiting for assembly to begin. M1 sat in between Nelson and Lisa. Mr Wilkinson came in with a woman none of them had seen before.

"Good morning, children."

"Good morning, Mr Wilkinson,"

chorused the school. "Good morning, everyone."

"Children, this is Mrs Ford who has come to our school to do a mini inspection, making sure that we're doing everything just right in our written work and the way we talk.

Now, as you all know, we *do* do everything just right so we have absolutely nothing to worry about, isn't that right, children?"

"Yes, Mr Wilkinson," chorused the children.

"So I want you to just go about your business as usual and be as helpful as possible. Will you do that?"

"Yes, Mr Wilkinson," chorused the children again.

"Good. Now go quietly back to your classrooms, please. Mrs Jeffries, would your class like to go first?"

The class stood up and followed their teacher out of the hall. M1 caught the inspector's eye and smiled. The inspector froze in horror and grabbed the head's arm.

79

"What is *that?*" she whispered, shaking. "That creature there? It looks like a dragon!"

"Oh, yes," said Mr Wilkinson, nervously. "That's M1, and he is indeed a dragon. The family live locally and he wanted to come to school desperately. He's turned out to be our very best pupil."

"A dragon in a school? Mr Wilkinson, what *can* you be thinking of? He'll have to go! You'll have to send for his parents immediately and get them to take him away once and for all."

"Oh, no," said the head. "I couldn't send him away – it would destroy the poor little chap. He absolutely loves school."

As the children left the hall some of them overheard the conversation. The word spread throughout the school that the inspector wanted M1 to be expelled.

"Don't tell M1," they whispered to each other. "He doesn't know and if he did he might get upset."

"Expelled indeed! We'll see about that!" declared Mrs Jeffries and she got M1 to come and stand in front of the class.

"Now, children, I am going to get M1 to blow some very small flames and I want you to write about fire. All right, M1, start blowing, please."

So M1 stood in front of the class blowing small orange and red and yellow and purple flames.

"Now, children, who can give me some good words to describe the colour of the flames?"

"Deep scarlet," cried one.

"Imperial purple," said another.

"Rich blue," called someone else.

"Luminous pink," came another response.

"Brilliant orange," contributed another.

"Excellent," said Mrs Jeffries, writing them up on the board. "And now describe the movement of the flames."

"Darting, flickering, shimmering, sparkling," came the responses.

"Excellent again," said Mrs Jeffries, writing them on the board too. "Now how about some smoke, M1."

M1 began blowing smoke just as the head and Mrs Ford the inspector walked in through the door. They stood at the back and watched.

"Some good words to describe the smoke now, children, to go with all these lovely words about flames."

"Grey."

"Drifting."

"Wafting."

"Curling elegantly."

"Wispy, cloudlike, teasing, dancing," cried different children.

"Wonderful!" declared Mrs Jeffries. "Now, I want you all to write a poem about fire and smoke, using the words on the board and any others you can think of. You too, M1."

The inspector watched the class working away in total silence and walked around looking at the poems.

"This is all excellent work, I'm very impressed," she said, and then she picked up M1's book and read his poem:

"Not to make flames,
Is one of my aims.
But when I do,
They're red, orange and blue."

"M1 in particular writes most poetically. Well, well, this *is* an unexpected sort of morning."

When the bell went and the inspector went off for a coffee, Mrs Jeffries breathed a sigh of relief "Well done, children," she said. "I'm proud of you."

After coffee the inspector went into another class, which had asked to borrow M1.

"This science lesson, children, is about fire," said the teacher. "Now M1 is going to breathe some fire for us and you can come up one at a time and feel the heat from the flames – not too close of course. Then I want you to tell me what we use fire for."

Soon there was a list on the board.

1. To keep warm
2. To cook with
3. To sterilize.
4. To look at: a lovely big fire in a dark room.
5. To generate electricity
6. To run steam engines
7. To light our way: candles lamps etc.

After that M1 helped the class boil water and test the temperature. Then he burned a bit of paper in front of the class and they discussed what happened to cause it to turn black and shrivel up into flakes. Then the teacher said, "Well, this *has* been an informative lesson, hasn't it? Now I want you all to tell me, one at a time, what you have learned this morning. Stacy, you start."

"You see how useful a school dragon is?" murmured the head, smiling, as he left the classroom with the inspector.

"I'm beginning to," said the inspector. "That class was having a most interesting discussion. I'm very impressed by their use of language."

That afternoon another class decided to put on a play and asked to borrow M1. All the school was invited to watch at the end of the day. Full of curiosity, the children trooped into the hall and sat down. At the back sat the teachers and the inspector. A boy came on to the stage carrying a sword and a shield with a big red cross on it.

"I am Saint George," he cried, "and this is my story. In a land far away there dwells a wicked dragon. This dragon eats fair maidens. I must go quickly to that land and kill this fiendish creature and rescue the fair maidens. Come with me on my journey."

Saint George jumped on a horse and rode off. He came to a royal palace where everyone was weeping and wailing, no one more loudly than the King and Queen.

"What's up?" asked Saint George.

"The dragon," wept the Queen.

"What is that evil animal doing now?"
demanded the knight.

"Our daughter, the beautiful Marianne – he wants to eat her! At this minute she is chained to a rock near the sea."

"Why are you giving her to the brute?" asked Saint George.

"He will burn up the whole land if we do not," the King told him and began to cry again.

"Never!" cried Saint George, waving his sword in the air. "I will rescue the princess – no problem."

The royals left and Saint George galloped off until he came to the princess hanging on the rock. All around children dressed as waves were wishing and washing near her. Then M1 came on looking very fierce.

"That princess is for me," he told Saint George. "Go away, I'm going to eat her."

"Never!" cried the knight. "I have come to rescue her."

M1 growled and snarled, "Then I'll eat you too, you silly knight."

M1 and Saint George had a very realistic fight, with lots of smoke and sparks and sword slashing. In the end M1 lay on the ground, pretending to be dead, and Saint George rescued the princess who agreed to marry him and live happily ever after.

"Hurray," yelled the children. Then M1 came on with some notes and began to read:

"On behalf of class 4W I would like to thank you for coming to watch our play and for listening so quietly. I would also like to point out that very few dragons are as horrible as the one that Saint George killed."

While the children clapped and cheered, the inspector turned to Mr Wilkinson and said, "I can see M1 is a great educational asset. I don't see how I could recommend that he be sent away – he really is such a delightful little chap and so enthusiastic. Yes, I think he should be allowed to stay in this school."

Chapter 6

The Nativity Play

Christmas came around and Mrs Jeffries was asked to put on the school nativity play. Mrs Jeffries gave everyone a part except M1.

"Isn't there a part for me?" the dragon asked sadly. "Even a very small part?"

"To be honest with you, M1, I'm not

at all sure what to do. You're by far the best reader in the class and you would be by far the best narrator."

M1's eyes shone with pleasure. "Oooh, I would love to be the narrator," he declared.

"I know," said Mrs Jeffries, "but I'd be constantly worrying in case you started a fire. With everyone on the stage acting and all the people in the audience, you might forget yourself and get excited. We can't risk a fire at an event like this. So I'm hoping you'll be my production assistant and help me backstage."

"Yes, all right," said M1, trying hard not to show his disappointment.

Jessie put her hand up. "Please, miss, it's not fair that M1 be left out. I mean, he was so brilliant in *Saint George and the Dragon*."

A murmur of agreement ran through the class.

"Miss, if I stood next to M1 right through the play with a bucket of water at the ready, could he be the narrator?" demanded Jessie.

"Don't you want to be in the play yourself, Jessie?"

"Not really, I hate acting. I like making the costumes and the scenery."

"Good," said the teacher. "Then Jessie can be the set designer and the wardrobe mistress and the fire-putter-outer, just in case M1 does get excited."

"Then can I read the Christmas story after all?" asked M1.

"Yes, M1, you certainly can."

M1 grinned from ear to ear. "I won't let you and the class down, Mrs Jeffries. I'll be the very best narrator you ever had."

Everyone worked very hard on the nativity play, making the set and the costumes and learning their lines. M1 read the story without a single mistake.

"Miss, we need a fire for the shepherds to sit round," Lisa pointed out one day. "Could the narrator come and be the fire for a minute?"

Mrs Jeffries laughed to herself. "Do you want to be the fire, M1?" she asked.

"Oooh, yes," said the dragon, and he put down the script and lay on the floor in the middle of the shepherds, gently blowing a few flames. Then Lisa (who was playing the Angel) came on and told them that Jesus had been born.

"You've all got to go to Bethlehem and tell him you're pleased he's here," she told them.

As the shepherds got up to go, M1 scrambled up and went back to the side of the stage to continue the story.

When the night of the play came, the school hall was packed with parents. Right at the back sat the dragon family; the caretaker stood nearby with a fire extinguisher in his hands. Mrs Dragon had bought a new hat and was sitting rather nervously clutching her handbag and keeping a careful eye on M2, M3, F1, F2 and little F3, who was sitting on her knee sucking a dummy. The young dragons, all dressed up in their best clothes, sat on the edge of their seats with just a tiny amount of smoke sneaking out of their nostrils.

The play started and when it came to the scene with the shepherds, M1 ran on to the stage. Then he lay on his back and gently breathed out tiny flames. The shepherds sat there warming their hands and moaning about the high taxes and

the bad weather. When the Angel came to tell them to go and follow the star, Nelson suddenly said, "We've got nothing to take the baby Jesus, but I bet it's cold in that stable. Let's take him our lovely fire, he'll like that."

"Good idea," said the other shepherds and they picked M1 up and carried him off.

"No!" whispered Mrs Jeffries urgently. "That's not in the script!"

But no one took any notice.

The scene changed to the stable. M1 came back on as the narrator, continued reading the story, and then ran off again. Mary sat holding Jesus, with Joseph standing behind her. There were a few cows and angels in the background. They were surrounded by straw. The shepherds walked in.

"You can look at the baby if you like," said Mary.

"He's lovely," the shepherds told her.

"We didn't have anything to bring the baby," Nelson said. "We're just poor shepherds. Then we thought it might be cold in a stable so we brought you a fire."

"That was a good idea," said Joseph.

"I was just saying to Mary that it was very cold in here."

"Yes, well, you just be careful where you put it. Keep it well away from the straw and the cows. From what I hear there are some kings coming this way and they're used to having their palaces all nice and warm."

"Yes," agreed Joseph. "They'll be well pleased."

The audience all roared with laughter and Mrs Jeffries breathed a huge sigh of relief.

M1 scrambled up and told the story of the three kings and then raced back to be the fire again. Then the three kings came on to the carol *We Three Kings of Orient Are,* and the audience joined in. They knelt before the baby and gave their gifts of gold, frankincense and myrrh. Then the kings went over to the fire.

"We've come a long way," they said. "Do you mind if we warm ourselves up a bit?"

"No, help yourselves," said Mary graciously.

"Thanks," replied one of the kings. "I'm getting on a bit and my knees are aching something terrible and a bit of a warm-up would do me good." And they went over to M1 who was lying on his back breathing out a few tiny red, orange and blue flames, as the audience laughed again.

"I've never seen an audience enjoy a nativity play so much," Mr Wilkinson whispered to Mrs Jeffries.

"I know," she agreed. "The children are making it up as they go along and it's very good."

M1 did his last reading and then everyone joined in singing *Away in a Manger*, while the shepherds and the kings knelt before the baby Jesus.

When the play was over the audience clapped and cheered. The performers joined hands and took a bow. M1 noticed his family at the back and waved.

Mr Dragon beamed proudly. "That's my boy," he told the caretaker. "The one that did all the reading and was the fire that warmed the baby Jesus."

"He took to it like a natural," the caretaker told Mr and Mrs Dragon. "I reckon school suits dragons."

"Ummm," mumbled Mr Dragon. "Yes, well, maybe."

"How do you do, Mr and Mrs Dragon and M2, M3, F1, F2 and F3?" said Mr

Wilkinson, coming over to them. "How nice to see you all here. Did you have a good time?"

"Oh, yes, thank you," chorused the little dragons. "And we would all like to come to your school, please, Mr Wilkinson."

"And I'd be happy to have you," Mr Wilkinson told them.

"Please, Daddy, please can we all go to school with M1?" begged the little dragons.

"I'll think about it," said Mr Dragon, smiling. "I really will."

"You may think about it as long as you please," interrupted Mrs Dragon. "But *my* mind is made up. These children get into no end of trouble at home all day. They're bored and they need something to do and this education seems a good thing to me."

Mr Dragon looked surprised. "I didn't know you felt that way, my love."

"Well, I do," his wife replied. "Ever since M1 went to school and has been able to read to us all, I've been thinking that all our children should be educated.

I like it when M1 reads me stories, and you like it when he reads the paper out to you."

Mr Dragon gave an embarrassed cough and let out a huge flame. The caretaker pointed the fire extinguisher at him.

"Well, if you insist, my dear, I suppose I'll have to say yes."

All the little dragons jumped up and down and cried, "Thank you Mummy, thank you Daddy, thank you Mr Head-teacher, thank you M1, thank you everyone! We're going to go to school!"

Jessie, Lisa and Nelson shouted, "Hurray, M1 can stay and all the little dragons are coming to school!"

Then M1 joined in, too: "Our school's a school for dragons!"

The End

The
Bad-Tempered
Dragon

JOAN LENNON

Illustrated by Serena Feneziani

For the Crumblies

Chapter 1

Black Cloaks and Woolly Jumpers

There once was a very junior wizard named Short and his companion who was a frog. Short was called Short because he wasn't very tall, and his companion was called Plantagenet because that was his name.

They went to Wizardry School.

Everyone knows that wizards are tall

and thin with great beaky noses. All the
Senior Wizards who taught at the school
looked like that, and most of the Junior
Wizard pupils did too. Short, on the other
hand, was small and weedy, and *his* nose
had freckles and turned up a little at the
end.

Wizards' companions are supposed to be sleek and superior-looking, like black cats or glossy ravens. They could often be quite bad-tempered as well, hissing or screeching at the drop of a pointy hat. But Plantagenet was bouncy and chatty and very, very green. And if *he* got mad, the worst anyone ever heard him say was a rather squeaky "Blarp".

Everyone knows that wizards always wear long black swirly cloaks while their companions sit up on their shoulders and look cross and proud. But Short wore warm woolly jumpers because you don't have to be much of a wizard to know that all frogs have very cold feet. And though companions usually have claws for holding on with, Plantagenet didn't, so that if Short stopped suddenly, *his* companion was likely to fall off.

When the class photo was taken, Short and Plantagenet were right there in the front row, looking short and woolly and green (at least, *Plantagenet* was looking green).

They were a strange pair.

The two went to Wizardry School in a large and prosperous town on the banks of the River Purpose. It was a fine town with

a shiny new supermarket full of special offers, a municipal fountain that was lit up by coloured lights in the evenings, and a Museum of Ancient Everything which nobody visited even though it was educational and good for you. Yet, in spite of all this, the town was not the sort of place to have stories told about it, because nothing exciting ever happened there. It was really rather dull. It was even called Dull – Dull-on-Purpose.

Dull was dull, until, out of the blue, something came to town that *was* worth telling a story about.

Chapter 2

"I'se Come to Stay!"

The something came sailing down the River Purpose on an empty, rather singed boat. The something was large and scaley and a sort of greeny-grey colour.

A few of the townspeople were fishing off the quay in a dull sort of way.

"What would you say that was?" asked one of them, looking upstream.

"Well . . . it's a, sort of a, what you might call a . . . boat. I think," someone answered.

"No, not the boat," said the first one. "It's the thing on the boat I can't quite place."

"Oh, the thing *on* the boat. Oh. Well. That's a . . . at least I think it's a . . . it's

bound to be a. . . Actually, I haven't a clue."

"Best ask it," someone suggested.

"Aye, it's sure to know," everyone agreed.

As the boat stopped sailing and bumped into the quay, the first fisher plucked up courage and called out,

"Er, excuse me, but what are you?"

The something belched fire at them and said, "I'se a bad-tempered dragon, I is, and I'se come to stay, and youse as don't like it is going to look round one day and find yourselves all overdone and crispy round the edges. So there."

This was so exciting that two of the fishers fell over backwards into the river in astonishment, as the Bad-Tempered Dragon stomped up the quay and headed for the town.

Wild rumours that something exciting was on its way spread all over town.

The Mayoress put on her best robe and chain and hurried out to welcome the dragon. The manager of Dull's shiny new supermarket straightened his tie, grabbed a handful of 2-for-1 coupons and raced to join her. The local branch of Mothers Against Everything was having morning coffee at Rosie's Café and turned out in force when the news reached them.

(They weren't Against Dragons at this point, but they *were* Against Missing Out on Anything.)

Soon everybody was trailing around after the Bad-Tempered Dragon, thinking How exciting! for at last something was really happening in Dull. But after a while, they started thinking How unpleasant! for the Bad-Tempered Dragon was appallingly badly-behaved.

Everyone knew that the Mayoress had been desperate to make a speech ever since she was elected thirty-six years ago, but nobody important ever came to Dull so she hadn't had a chance.

"Welcome to wonderful Dull," she said now in her plummiest Mayoress voice, as all the townspeople smiled proudly, "our lovely, large and prosperous town situated on the River —"

But that was as far as she got. The Bad-Tempered Dragon didn't listen He didn't even try to look interested. Instead he gave a huge bored yawn, blowing black soot all over the Mayoress's glasses and setting her notes on fire.

"P. . . P. . . P. . ." spluttered the Mayoress, and the Bad-Tempered Dragon stomped on.

"Excuse me, excuse me," called the manager of the supermarket as he tried to catch up. "Could I interest you in our 2-for-1 Bonanza Extra-Special Special Offer?"

The Bad-Tempered Dragon stopped a moment and looked at the handful of Bonanza Extra-Special Special 2-for-1 coupons the manager was waving at him. Then he ate them.

The manager was so surprised he just stood there with his mouth open, as the Bad-Tempered Dragon stomped on up to his shiny new supermarket and through the automatic front doors.

Then the Bad-Tempered Dragon had a chew on everything in sight, including the Special Offer signs. He went joy-riding on all the supermarket trolleys, and bent their frames so that not only would they not go straight, they wouldn't go at all. He turned the Fresh Bread Department into the Burnt Toast Department, and the Frozen Food Department into the Defrosted and Then Some Department. And when a nice lady in a frilly apron politely offered him some little cubes of cheese on toothpicks, he didn't even say thank you, and he did melt the tray they were on.

The manager went home with a headache and the Bad-Tempered Dragon stomped on.

Dull had a beautiful municipal fountain in its fine Town Square which was lit up every evening with coloured lights. And by the time the Bad-Tempered Dragon had finished with that, two-thirds of the members of Mothers Against Everything had fainted, and the Secretary was already starting on her third sign Forbidding *Anyone* to Dabble their Fingers in Municipal Fountains Ever Again.

Then the Bad-Tempered Dragon was tired. He went to Dull's best hotel and made them bring all the duvets and all the pillows from all the bedrooms into the Grand Ballroom, which *he* said was the only place big enough for him to sleep in.

And when Dull's Golden Trotters Dancing Club (who had only just caught up with the crowd) very politely reminded him that tomorrow at 9.00 a.m. sharp they were meant to be learning the Samba, he made rude noises at them.

The townspeople looked at each other in horror.

"What shall we do?" someone asked.

They all scratched their heads and thought hard.

"Um. . ." said someone.

"Er. . ." said someone else.

"Well. . ." said someone else again.

"AhHA!" said the voice of a little old lady at the back of the crowd. "I've got it!"

Everyone turned to look. In fact the sight of all those townspeople staring at once made the idea (which had to do with knitting an enormous cage and putting the dragon *and* the Grand Ballroom in it and then somehow getting wheels underneath and rolling the whole lot into the river at midnight, and therefore *probably* wouldn't have worked anyway) go right out of her brain.

"Or . . . or perhaps a *better* idea," quavered the little old lady, who was now blushing furiously, "would be to go and ask the Wizards."

The townspeople looked at each other again. Wizards, good for something? Then, as one, they headed for the School of Wizardry.

Chapter 3
The Attack of the Senior Wizards

Next morning, the most Senior Wizard called the entire school to assembly. She was extremely tall and incredibly thin and had a nose that would have made an eagle envious. She was not a Headteacher who had problems with discipline.

She stood at the front of the hall in her

black clothes for a long, dramatic moment. Then she said in a shivery voice,

"Ridding a Large and Prosperous Town of Bad-Tempered Dragons."

There was another long, dramatic pause. Then,

"Watch and learn!" said the most Senior Wizard as she swirled her black cloak and strode off.

The other Senior Wizards swirled *their* black cloaks and strode after her.

And all the Junior Wizards clattered up the stairs to the very top tower for a better view.

Dull's School of Wizardry looked out over the town from the top of a hill, and the top tower of the school was an excellent place for getting fresh air and keeping an eye on the neighbours at the same time. For a long while, however,

everything seemed peaceful below. Then,
"Look!" called one of the Junior
Wizards.

A plume of smoke was moving above the streets that led from the River Purpose.

The Bad-Tempered Dragon was returning from his bath. The Junior Wizards could hear him humming, terribly out of tune, as he reached the Town Square and stretched out in the sun to dry.

Then the Junior Wizards began to nudge one another excitedly and point. Creeping up along one of the side streets, they could see the most Senior Wizard. And even from this distance, they could see that the jar she was holding was full of something very bubbly, very wizardly, and very purple.

Then Short nudged Plantagenet. On another side street was a sword and a disgruntled-looking raven, travelling along in mid-air without any visible means of support.

"Invisibility Spell Number 6," said Short.

"He forgot the last instruction," snorted Plantagenet.

"What's that?" asked Short.

"Thou shalt not pick anything up after ye spell is complete —"

"No, *that*! and what's *THAT*!" Short was pointing to another side street, and then another.

Converging on the Town Square, along the dozens of little streets, were dozens of Senior Wizards. They came clutching potions and powders, cloaks and ropes, dragon-proofed brooms and magical toothbrushes.

The Junior Wizards looked at each other in amazement. This was going to be worth watching.

There was a moment of absolute stillness, and then it began.

"KA-BLAMM!"

"Have at thee!"

"Take that, foul serpent!"

"One, two, out goes you!"

"By hook or by crook, I'll bop you with this book!"

"CRASH!"

"BANG!"

"Ooops!"

"Sorry. . ."

Purple smoke filled the Square, pierced by flashes of lightning and the odd stray firework. Soon the Junior Wizards couldn't see *what* was going on, though they could hear plenty of thumping

and coughing, and the sound of people
falling over each other.

Then,

"RoarRRRR!" said the Bad-Tempered
Dragon. "Youse is pestering me. When I
is counted to five I want youse GONE.
I'se counting now. One – six – three –
FIVE!"

The Bad-Tempered Dragon was not good at counting, but it didn't seem to matter. As the purple smoke began to clear, they could see that there were *no* wizards left in the Town Square.

There was only the sound of sniggering, as the Bad-Tempered Dragon lay in the sun.

As the Junior Wizards came down from the top tower, they were strangely quiet. If the best efforts of the tallest and thinnest of the school's most Senior Wizards only succeeded in making the Bad-Tempered Dragon laugh, what hope did Dull have?

Chapter 4

"Don't Drop That Jar!"

The next morning, late, the whole school was called to assembly once more.

The most Senior Wizard stood at the front of the hall. Her black cloak was tattered, she had purple smudges in her hair, and her eyebrows had been singed off. The other Senior Wizards didn't look much better.

"Until further notice," said the most Senior Wizard in a tired voice, "everyone's assignment is as follows: 'Ridding . . . ahem . . . a Large and Prosperous Town of Bad-Tempered Dragons.' Anyone with questions will find us in the Senior Wizards' Staff-room."

The Senior Wizards limped off, and all the Junior Wizards raced for the labs to start their exciting new assignment.

Short tried to race too, but unfortunately Plantagenet wasn't ready and immediately fell over backwards. By the time they'd sorted themselves out and reached the labs, all the cauldrons

and most of the jars of purple stuff had already been spoken for. All around them there was a babble of spelling and mis-spelling as Junior Wizards settled to their work.

Plantagenet and Short looked at one another.

"Maybe there's something left at the back of the cupboards. You try that one, and I'll look here," said Short.

Plantagenet nodded and hopped off.

Wizard cupboards are well known for having strange and wonderful things overlooked at the back of them, but Short didn't have much luck with his. The dust that was getting in his hair and up his nose wasn't very strange, or wonderful either. He was sneezing so hard he had to come out of the cupboard and sit down.

Suddenly Plantagenet called. Short couldn't see him at first, but then there was the frog, backing out of another cupboard, clutching a jar. He called again,

"I'm here! Over here!"

He sounded really excited.

Something whispered *Trouble!* in Short's brain. Something whispered *Lunchtime!* in Short's stomach. This always happened when he was nervous.

"And bring some water with you!" called Plantagenet. Reluctantly Short did as he was told.

"Pour it into the jar," said the frog. Short tried to read the label at the same time, but it was so old and cobwebby he couldn't tell what it said.

"Now look deep into the jar," ordered Plantagenet, "and tell me what you see."

Short looked. He saw nothing but a sort of sludge. His heart sank.

166

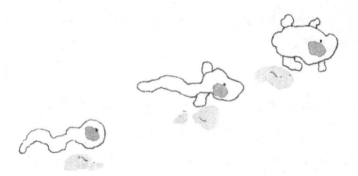

"Oh, Plantagenet," he groaned. "This isn't going to be like watching your home movies, is it? Not 'This is me as a tadpole', 'This is me just before I lost my tail', 'This is —'"

"Look deeper, Short!" interrupted Plantagenet. "This is no ordinary sludge. It isn't even the very special sludge from my own home pond. You are looking at Prehistoric Sludge!"

"Excuse me?" said Short, but Plantagenet's already bulging eyes were starting to pop out of his head.

The sludge in the jar
had begun to steam.

"Oh-oh," said Plantagenet.

"What do you mean, 'Oh-oh'?" said
Short in a worried voice.

"Maybe you shouldn't have added the
water just yet," said Plantagenet.

Short was starting to say, "But you told
me to!" when Plantagenet thrust the
steaming jar into his hands and hopped up
on to his shoulder.

"Let's go!" urged the
frog, holding on tight
to Short's ear.

They raced from the lab, scattering startled Junior Wizards as they went, and tumbled out into the street.

"But where are we going?" panted Short.

"To the Museum of Ancient Everything," was the answer, "and DON'T DROP THAT JAR!"

Chapter 5

Short Scales the Heights

Inside the Museum it was still and dim. Plantagenet peered at the floor plan and then hustled Short down a corridor to the Great Hall.

"The Bad-Tempered Dragon!" gasped Short, but it was only a huge skeleton. A huge dinosaur skeleton.

The thing loomed over them out of

the shadows. Somehow the word "big" just didn't seem big enough.

"All right, Short, it's up to you now," whispered Plantagenet.

"What?!" squeaked Short, and back came a horrible squeaky echo from high up in the Great Hall. *"What?! What?!"*

"Somebody's got to get the Prehistoric Sludge into the dinosaur's mouth," insisted Plantagenet. "And you're the tallest somebody here."

Short stared at him.

"And could I just add," said the frog, "that you've very little time left. This sludge is due to go off in three minutes and forty-two seconds, exactly."

"Go off?" said Short. He was puzzled. "You mean it's going to go bad?"

"No," answered Plantagenet. "I mean, it's going to explode."

Short looked at the frog. He looked at the jar. He looked at the head of the skeleton, high above. All the things that had whispered *Trouble!* and *Lunchtime!* to him before had stopped whispering. Now they were shouting, *Get out! Get out!*

Short gulped.

"This is no time to get cold feet!" screeched Plantagenet.

"Look who's talking!" snapped Short, who was trying to think.

The frog was hopping up and down so fast he blurred. "Use a spell! Use a potion! Use an incantation!"

"Use a table," said Short, shortly.

"Oh," said Plantagenet, and he stopped hopping and came as close to blushing as anyone as green as that could. "Right. Good idea."

Huffing and puffing, Short pushed a table over from the wall to under the skeleton's head, and climbed up.

Not tall enough.

Puffing and panting, he heaved a chair on to the table, and climbed up.

Still not tall enough.

Knees shaking, Short up-ended a metal wastepaper bin, pushed it on to the table, piled it on to the chair, and climbed up.

It was just tall enough

"You could hurt yourself messing about on a contraption like that," said Plantagenet, from a safe distance away on the floor.

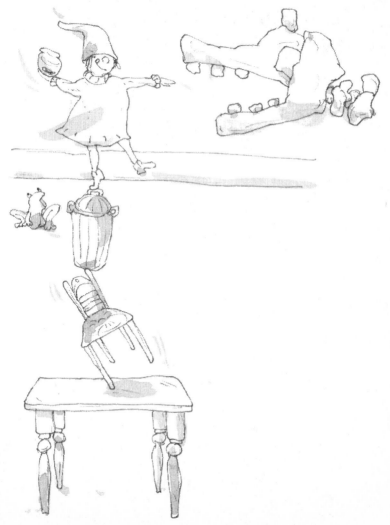

Short, who was holding a jar due to explode in fifteen and a half seconds, exactly, did not answer. He just gritted his teeth to stop them chattering, balanced as well as he could on top of the bin, and, at full stretch, tipped the sludge into the skeleton's mouth.

Then he fell off the bin, the chair, *and* the table.

For the skeleton had moved.

"That was delicious," it said. "Got any more?"

Short was on the floor trying to rub all his bumped bits, but Plantagenet boldly hopped forward and said, "Sorry, that's it."

"Too bad," said the skeleton regretfully. "Now, how can I help?"

Chapter 6

Cracking Down on the Egg

Outside in the sunlight, the Bad-Tempered Dragon had discovered Dull's children's playground. His eyes gleamed. He kicked all the sand out of the sand-pit, bent the climbing frames, and snapped the see-saw. He was just about to use the chains from the swings to floss his teeth, when he heard an unexpected sound.

Thud! Thud!

The Bad-Tempered Dragon turned a paler greeny-grey. The ground was trembling.

Thud! Thud!

Suddenly it stopped. The Bad-Tempered Dragon fearfully turned his head. His jaw dropped, then he shrieked and covered his face with his claws.

"*Well!*" said a disgusted voice. "That an egg of an egg of an egg of mine should behave like this!"

The Bad-Tempered Dragon looked about him at the wreckage, and burped an apologetic flame.

"Say excuse me. And cover your mouth."

"Yes, Greater-than-Great-Grandmama," whispered the Bad-Tempered Dragon.

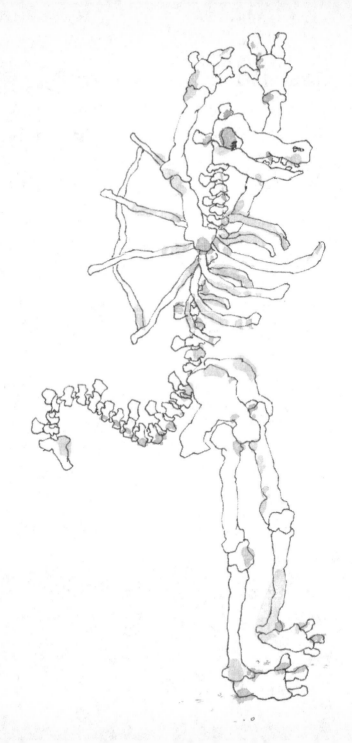

"And tidy this mess."

"Yes, Greater-than-Great-Grandmama."

"And the hotel and the supermarket, whatever they are. And make sure you CLEAN OUT THE FOUNTAIN!"

The Bad-Tempered Dragon hung his head, blushed a rather dingy brown, and said in a voice you could hardly hear,

"Yes, Greater-than-Great-Grandmama. Sorry."

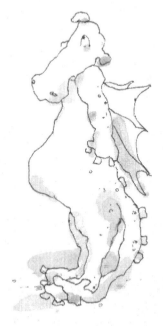

"I should think so. Evolution has a lot to answer for, if you ask me. Oh, and give the Museum of Ancient Everything a dust while you're at it. Especially the Great Hall."

And the enormous skeleton looked down at Short and Plantagenet, standing carefully clear of her big feet, and smiled.

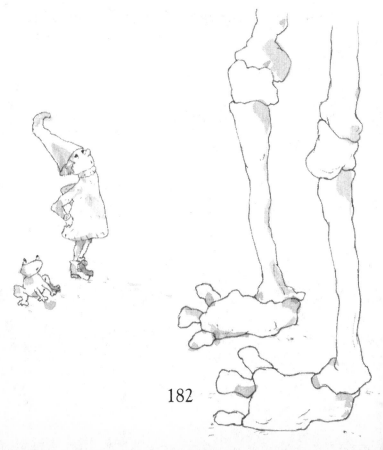

Then, all of a sudden, she opened her huge, boney mouth wide. For one horrible moment, Short thought she was about to swallow them, but the Bad-Tempered Dragon's Greater-than-Great-Grandmama was only yawning.

"Delicious sludge, that," she said, "but it's wearing off. I'll be getting back now. But any more trouble and. . ."

She glared meaningfully at the dejected dragon, and then stomped back to the Museum of Ancient Everything, and another well-earned rest.

After that, the Bad-Tempered Dragon was a changed creature. At first he behaved better because he was terrified Plantagenet and Short might bring his Greater-than-Great-Grandmama back again. But after a while, behaving well grew into a habit, and he gradually became known as the Well-Tempered Dragon.

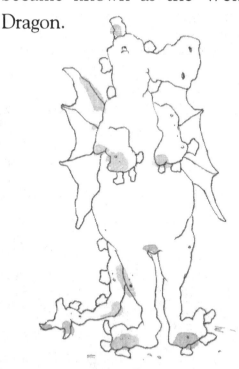

He became very fond of the Museum of Ancient Everything and liked stomping about dusting things in it. He took particularly good care of the Great Hall.

Short and Plantagenet were heroes. Now when the class photo was taken, all the other Junior Wizards were wearing woolly jumpers, and all the other companions were trying to look bouncy and not using their claws to hold on.

The Mayoress ordered that a statue of Short climbing up to the dinosaur's mouth, with Plantagenet encouraging him, should be made. A famous modern sculptor came all the way from somewhere important to do it. The local

branch of Mothers Against Everything insisted that there be a sign nearby saying "Don't Try This at Home". But because the statue was so *very* modern, it wasn't clear what was happening, so there wasn't much danger.

Short and Plantagenet continued to make a wizard good team, even though the boy never did get much taller, and the frog never became less green.

And the townspeople of Dull were happy. For although their town was once again not the sort to have stories told about it, as a place to live in it was much more pleasant.

The End

The Little
Pet Dragon

PHILIPPA GREGORY

Illustrated by David Wyatt

For Victoria and Adam

Chapter 1

James Alastair lived in a small red-brick house, part of a terrace of houses in a little town beside the North Sea. All his life he had wanted a greyhound. Greyhounds are long lean dogs: tremendously fast runners that are sometimes trained to be racers and win prizes for their owners. James Alastair dreamed of owning a racing greyhound. He dreamed of owning the fastest greyhound in the world.

One day – the day before his ninth birthday – James was walking along the street on his way home from school, wondering what his mother and father would give him for his present. He knew it would not be a greyhound, and he was afraid that it would not be a bicycle either. Everyone in his class had a bicycle except James. Suddenly, he stopped.

There, on the pavement in front of him, was a wooden basket – the sort that gardeners use for carrying small plants and trowels. Inside it, coiled up very small, was a little animal. It had a little snouty face like a tiny crocodile, but much smileyer. It had

round nostrils and loving, deep amber eyes. It had two sharp ears that stood up, rather like a horse's. It had a fat little body covered in scales and a long, long tail like nothing in the world. Running down its spine was a row of hard, triangle-shaped spikes. Its plump feet had sharp golden claws. It was a bright emerald green. It was shimmering all over with the light of a very strong magic spell. James could hardly see it for the power of the magic spell. Instead he saw the very thing he wanted most in the world.

"A greyhound!" James said in absolute wonder. "A greyhound puppy!"

James bent down and stroked the dragon's hard snouty head, but he did not feel scales – he felt soft, silky fur. The dragon looked up at him adoringly and tried to wag its tail in a greyhound-like way. James smoothed under its chin where its softer skin was a pale lime colour and felt a string tied around its neck. On the string was a label, and on the label was some black, spiky, magical-looking writing. It said:

Please look after this little Pet Dragon.
I made him by accident and now
he needs a home.
You can name him whatever you like.
signed

Meehort the Wizard

James rubbed his eyes and read the label again. But even as he was reading it the letters were swimming around like fish in a pond. The second time he read it, the message was completely different:

Please look after this little greyhound puppy. He has no mother or father, and he needs a home. You can name him whatever you like.

signed

Meehort the Wizard

Of course, James was delighted. He picked up the gardener's basket with the small green dragon inside. It was very light, no heavier than a greyhound puppy. He carried it home in his arms and put it carefully on the kitchen table.

His mother and father were out. James thought carefully about what they might say when they saw his surprising new pet. He rather hoped they would be absolutely delighted. He rather knew that they would not.

James put his head on one side and looked at the little dragon. He saw the most beautiful fawn-coloured greyhound puppy. The dragon put *its* head on one side too and looked back at James. It saw a nine-year-old boy (well, very nearly nine), rather small for his age, with a dirty face and a wide smile with a gap where a tooth was missing.

"You're my greyhound puppy," James said to him. "I'm going to keep you whatever anyone says."

Just then, the back door opened and his mother came in from the garden. James hastily pulled a tea towel over his new pet's snouty little head. All that showed was one marigold eye.

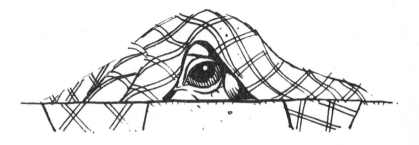

"What on earth are you doing with that trug?" asked James's mother. "I've just wiped the table."

The little green dragon hidden under the tea towel looked surprised. He didn't mind being called a greyhound but you could tell from the hurt look in his rose-amber eyes that he didn't like being called a trug.

"Look, Mam!" James said, paying no attention to the wiping of the table or the trug. "A greyhound puppy!" He flung back the tea towel and the little dragon sat up.

James's mother looked in the basket and her face went warm and tender. The magician's magic was wonderfully powerful. All she saw was a fawn-coloured greyhound puppy with long legs and intelligent eyes.

"Isn't he sweet," she said. "I wonder who he belongs to?"

The dragon tried to wag its tail like a greyhound puppy.

"Can I keep it?" James asked. "Can I please, Mam? For my birthday? *Please?*"

James's dad had not had a job since the steel mill near their home had closed down. James's mam had to work as a cleaner at an office block at night to earn enough money for the three of them. And there never was enough money, however hard she worked. She had been worrying all day about James's birthday. They did not have enough money to buy him a bicycle so they would have to give him something else, something cheaper, and he would have to pretend to like it. The same thing had happened last year as well.

It made her want to cry when she had to say "no" to James. It made her face look sad and pale when she had to work late at night, pushing a heavy floor polisher over the wooden floor. It made James's dad feel so helpless and so angry that he wanted to dash into the steel mill and open it up and make steel all on his own. But of course he could not. It made all three of them miserable.

"We can't afford to feed him," she said. It was true. They had hardly enough money to feed themselves, and they never had any treats. They never had steak or ice-cream or cakes from the shop. They never had holidays away from home.

The dragon bunched itself up to look tiny, and peered up at James's mother. His little green face seemed to promise that he would eat hardly a thing.

As he moved, James saw something glinting in the basket under the dragon. He pulled it out. It was a large golden guinea coin from the olden days. Stuck to it, with a blob of red sealing-wax marked with a special magic-looking seal, was another note in the spiky black handwriting, that said:

This is for his keep. He can eat dog food if you insist. But he likes flowers in Summertime.

This was all rather odd. And the oddest thing of all was that James's mother didn't seem a bit surprised.

"There's your dad's garden in flower all the summer long," she said.

James's father was a brilliant gardener. Their street backed on to the allotments where there was a huge old derelict greenhouse. It had once been the greenhouse in the gardens of a grand manor house. But now the gardens had become allotments and the greenhouse was empty and just used as a store. Everyone in the street had an allotment and grew vegetables.

James's dad was different. He grew the vegetables that they needed for eating, but all around the borders of the vegetable patch he grew flowers. He loved flowers. He grew roses and daisies, chrysanthemums, great big ragged-headed dahlias, and small, sweet-smelling lilies of the valley. His favourite flowers were the wild and wonderful orchids that will only grow in the islands of the South Seas. James's dad would look at pictures of orchids in books and dream about growing them.

It was an impossible dream, for orchids have to be kept very warm and the only place James's dad had for delicate plants was the kitchen window-sill. Indeed, all the window-

sills in James's house were already crowded with pots with little shoots growing in them.

"The gold coin will pay for his dog food!" James said excitedly. "So can we keep him, Mam? Can we? For my birthday?"

James's mam looked from James's excited face to the dragon's appealing little eyes.

"Yes!" she said suddenly. "Why not!"

All at once James felt reckless and brave.

Why not? Why *shouldn't* they do something exciting and daring that would make them all feel happy?

"*Yes!*" he shouted, and he dashed out to the allotment, to find his dad and tell him that they had a pet – a wonderful greyhound puppy who might grow up to be a champion racer.

"He certainly has the looks for it," his dad said when he came in, all breathless, with James tugging at his muddy hand. "See how intelligent his eyes are?" The little dragon's eyes went dark with happiness from a yellowy amber until they were red as coals with his eagerness.

"See how long and thin his body is?" said James's dad. "That's a good sign."

The little dragon stretched out to his full length. His spiky tail hung over the edge of the basket. It had a hard little triangle at the end. But it was very powerful magic indeed, for no one saw a dragon at all. They all saw a greyhound puppy.

"He's a champion!" James's dad said.

He lifted the little dragon out of the trug and put him gently down on the kitchen floor. The little dragon waddled over to where the central heating boiler stood in the corner of the kitchen. It was warm and it hummed softly. Perhaps it reminded him of the inside of his eggshell when he was a little baby dragon, not yet hatched. He flumped down on the floor beside it and smiled at them with his rosy eyes all misty and contented.

"We'll get him a dog basket and keep it there," James's mam said, pleased. "I'll give him a box just for now."

They found a cardboard box for him, and lined it with one of James's dad's old holey jumpers. The dragon sat quietly in the box as if he had lived with them all his life.

"Tomorrow," James's mam said, "we'll take him to the vet for his injections."

Chapter 2

The visit to the vet was not a great success.

"This is a very strange sort of dog. What breed is it?" asked the vet, looking very sternly at James and his mam over the top of her spectacles. "I have never seen such a dog in my life before."

The dragon curled up tighter in his basket and looked at her with anxious yellow eyes.

"We thought it was a greyhound puppy," James's mam said.

The vet shook her head. "Definitely not," she said.

Magic does not seem to work very well on vets. She could see that he was not a pedigree greyhound, but she could not see exactly what he was.

"He must be some kind of mongrel," she said.

The vet ran her skilled hands over the dragon and she felt fur. She pulled at the hard scaly skin at the dragon's neck and tried to inject him. The needle broke at once and the injection liquid squirted into James's hair.

"Gracious!" said the vet, amazed. "That must be a faulty needle. I *am* sorry. Are you all right?"

"Yes!" said James. "Yes, yes."

The dragon's little face looked old and wise. He had not understood what they wanted to do to him. Now he knew. When the vet had the next injection ready he quickly stretched so that there was a tiny opening between the scales on his neck. The needle slipped in easily. He let out a little squeak (baby dragons are not very brave) and James rubbed his head.

"There," the vet said. "Don't let him walk on the pavements until he has had a booster shot."

The little pet dragon's eyes went quite primrose with dismay at this, but he sat very still in his basket while James carried it out of the surgery to the bus stop.

"It *is* my birthday today, Mam," he said quietly at the bus stop. "Even if he is a mongrel you won't take him away from me, will you?"

His mam sniffed. "I don't think she knew what she was talking about," she said defiantly. "He looks like a greyhound to your dad and me. He'll be a greyhound to us. What shall we call him?"

James thought for a moment. Ever since the vet had doubted that his pet was a real true bred pedigree greyhound he had been wanting to give him a real doggy name, to make it clear to everyone what he was.

"Lassie," he said. "We'll call him Lassie the Wonder Dog."

That should settle any doubts, he thought, pleased. No one could doubt that his pet was a true-bred dog if he answered to the name of Lassie the Wonder Dog.

Lassie the little pet dragon soon learned to come when he was called. He learned to walk to heel. He learned to fetch sticks. He tried his best to bark. When he went out for a walk with James or his dad or his mam he walked on a lead and sat at the kerb while they waited to cross the road. Never in the entire history of dragons did a little green dragon try harder to be a dog.

And it worked. It might have been magic, or it might have been that people just don't expect to see dragons walking nicely to heel or tied to the lamppost outside the corner shop. Pretty soon everyone in the streets all around James's home knew that Lassie was James's dog and that he might one day be a prizewinning racing greyhound.

Spring came, and James's dad decided that they could start Lassie's training. Every afternoon, after school, James, his dad and Lassie would go to the wide, flat stretch of grass which ran between the sea wall and the sea road. In summertime all the men would bring their dogs out there to race them, one against the other. They had a little machine – a box with an engine and a long rope which pulled a bundle of cloth very quickly in front of the racing dogs. The dogs all thought it was a hare or a rabbit and chased after it. The winner was the first one past the finishing line.

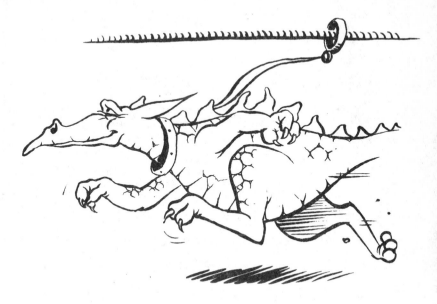

James and his dad started training Lassie by running alongside him, but he was much too fast for them. In the end they stretched out a long rope and James stood at one end and his dad at the other. They clipped Lassie's lead to the rope to make sure that he could not get away, and then they called Lassie from one end to the other.

Every evening James and his dad and Lassie
went for their training session by the sea wall.
As the weather grew warmer, the big waves
rolling in and breaking on the beach on the
far side of the wall changed colour from iron

grey to blue, and the cold wind that blew off the sea grew warmer and gentler. Very soon Lassie was running from James to his dad and back again without a rope or a lead. Soon they could take him down to the wide dry sand of the beach and let him run and run and run.

No one had seen a young dog run as fast or as far as Lassie. Every day he got faster and faster. He grew sleek and well muscled, his chest grew wider, his tummy grew slimmer and his eyes shone. He gave up eating tinned dog food and started eating flowers. James's dad brought him the fading heads of daffodils, and then the bluebells from the little garden.

When summer came and the allotment
borders were filled with flowers, Lassie was
allowed out to graze on whatever he liked. He
never ate the buds, and if James's dad asked
him to leave one particular plant alone, he
never forgot. They had a tiny patch of grass in
the back garden and James did not have to
mow it once that summer. The dragon went
along it, nibbling away at the tops of the grass
and the daisy petals.

By the middle of June, Lassie looked like a beautiful dog in the prime of condition. A lot of the men who owned racing greyhounds had seen him in training and they kept asking James and his dad to come along one evening and race Lassie against their dogs. James used to love to see his dad smile and put them off. "When the time is right," he said wisely. "He's a young dog as yet. We don't want to rush him."

"I think you have a proper champion on your hands there," one of the men told him. "You bring him for a race against our dogs and if he wins we'll all help you train him. He'd be a credit to us."

James's dad finally agreed. "Next month, then," he said.

Chapter 3

Every kid in James's school came to the sea front to watch Lassie race. It was nearly the end of the school term and it felt as if the summer holidays had come early. Every mam who had nothing better to do that day strolled out to see Lassie race, and they brought the little kids in their pushchairs and the babies in their prams. An ice-cream van

saw the crowd and stopped on the sea road
and played the tune so loudly that all the
kids with pocket money queued up for ice-
creams, and those that didn't have any
money swapped everything they could think
of for a lick.

Every man who owned a greyhound, or
had once had a greyhound, or thought he
might get one some day, was there. Some of
the very old men could remember when the
little town had bred a champion greyhound
before, and they kept taking people by the
arm and telling them all about it. It was quite
a crowd and in the centre of it all, envied by
everyone, smiling so wide that you could see
the gap in his teeth, was James holding Lassie

on a beautiful new red collar and lead which his mam had given him last night. She had been saving up for it for three weeks.

Lassie's eyes were bright and alert. His ears pricked up with excitement. He understood exactly what they wanted him to do and he loved running races. He was so excited that he could feel a hot smoky feeling building up inside him. He gave a little gasp and a tiny cloud of smoke puffed out of his nostrils. Lassie sniffed it back inside quickly, before anyone noticed. He knew very well that promising young greyhounds do not breathe fire.

James knelt down beside him and lovingly pulled his ears. "Now don't get frightened," he said. "Just try your hardest. If you don't win, it doesn't matter. We just want to see how well you do."

The little dragon's heart burned with love. He had to hold his breath to stop the smoke leaking out. He looked at James with his warm amber eyes. Nothing in the world

could stop him winning the race, he thought. He was absolutely determined to win the race for James.

There was a race for other dogs before it was Lassie's turn. James turned to watch them. The men put their dogs into a row of little boxes, fastened the doors, and stepped back. The dogs looked out through the front of the boxes, some of them whining with excitement and eagerness. Someone started the machine which whipped away the little bundle of cloth down the grass. The front doors of the boxes all flew open together and the dogs raced down the track, chasing the cloth, towards the machine where their owners caught them.

"If he wins here we could enter him at a proper greyhound racing track," James's dad said. "We could go all around the country, racing with him. And he could win money too. A prizewinning greyhound is a wonderful animal. He'll get his picture in the papers. We'll be famous."

Lassie could feel the heat burning and burning inside him. There was a cool breeze blowing gently off the sea. He turned his nose towards it and let out a little puff of smoke. He was so excited he could hardly bear to wait.

"Our turn now," James's dad said at last. "You can put him in the hutch, James."

Very gently James directed Lassie into the hutch. Lassie peered out through the grille at the front. He could see James and James's dad walking up to the finishing line. He could see James's mam standing with her friends. He could see all the kids from James's school getting ready to cheer. He could feel a huge smoky excited warmth growing in his tummy, and then he could feel a strange itchy bursty feeling on either shoulder.

He tried to concentrate on what was happening. Someone was resetting the machine, then they pulled the little bundle of cloth towards the hutches and the other dogs barked and whined. Lassie couldn't quite see the point of chasing a duster, but it was obvious that James wanted him to chase it, so he would. Someone shouted "Ready?" And someone else called back "Ready!" Then the grille on the front of the hutch flew

open and Lassie leaped out.

He was ahead of the other dogs in a few quick strides. The bundle of cloth was whizzing away from him. Lassie put down his sleek head and raced after it, his paws pounding on the smooth turf. The legs of the school kids, the wheels of the pushchairs, the feet of the grown-ups all flashed past him as he ran faster than he had ever run before. He could feel his breath coming in hot smoky

gasps, and his heart pounding faster than his paws. Then there was a rush and a bang and he was at the finish line and he heard James's excited yell: "Lassie! Oh, Lassie! You won!"

But he was too excited to stop, and the smoking feeling in his tummy was too hot, and the itchy feelings on his shoulders were too much for him. He ran past James, diving under his outstretched hands. He dashed on and on, down the sea front, unstoppable, uncatchable, the fastest greyhound that there had ever been in the history of the world. And as he ran he heard a wonderful powerful ripple of sound as two curtains of green wings finally burst from his shoulders and opened on either side of his body. Then he was not running any more but his feet were racing through air, and the ground was falling away below him and the salty cool wind was buoying him upwards and upwards.

His wings were beating strongly and smoothly and Lassie the little pet dragon was a fully-fledged dragon – flying free, soaring, as high as a party balloon, as high as a kite, as high as a glider, as high as an aeroplane – higher, higher, higher, past small surprised sparrows, past soaring seagulls, past all the birds until he was a little black dot circling high in the pale evening sky.

"Lassie!" James yelled, suddenly afraid, suddenly terrified. "Lassie! Come back! Don't leave me Lassie! Don't go!"

In utter horror James watched his pet – the pet that only a moment ago was certain to be a champion greyhound – circle and turn in the empty sky. James watched him soar and wheel, as if to get his bearings, and then he beat his wings strongly and headed away, away from the sea front, away from the cold chimneys of the derelict steel mill, away from James's little house with the allotments and the old greenhouse behind it, away towards the west and the setting sun.

James forgot about his friends and all the grown-ups who were staring open-mouthed at the sky. He threw himself face down on the grass and wept as if his heart was breaking.

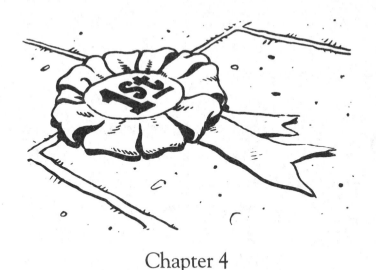

Chapter 4

James did not go home at once, he felt too miserable. While his mam and dad walked slowly home, arm in arm, very quiet and sad, and everyone else stood around at the sea front chattering and pointing in the air and marvelling at what they had just seen, James went the long way round, by the back alleys where no one would see him and notice his red eyes and muddy face. Surely no one in the whole world was ever as unlucky! No one ever before could have found a prizewinning champion greyhound puppy and then watch it turn into a small dragon and fly away.

If he had run off like an ordinary dog, or even been run over by a car, James might have felt better. But the picture in his mind of his pet circling higher and higher and flying towards the sunset was so painful that it was well after teatime before he had cried enough on his own and felt able to go home and face the sympathy of his mam and dad.

But when he came around the corner into his street he knew at once that something else had happened. His dad was out in the street staring up at the sky, and all the neighbours were out too. The whole street seemed to be there, looking upwards and pointing. The little kids were jumping up and down and yelling encouragement. But the grown-ups were looking worried. James rubbed the last of the tears from his face and ran up to his dad and pulled at his sleeve.

"It's Lassie," Dad said, his hand shielding his eyes from the setting sun as he squinted upwards. He didn't even glance down at James. "He's having trouble landing. He tried to land in the street but he clipped the lamppost. He seems to have grown very big."

James felt like leaping in the air himself. His pet was coming home like a huge green homing pigeon! Lassie had not run away – he

was coming home to where he belonged. It was wonderful. It was as big a miracle as finding him in the first place. Lassie wanted to come back. It was magic!

"Look out!" James's dad yelled suddenly. "Here he comes!"

People screamed and ran for their front doors. Lassie loomed down on them like a great green airship. James could see the pale green of his big belly, his claws outstretched as if he were trying to grab on to the air to slow himself up. James could see his wide frightened eyes as he scorched overhead. A few panicky puffs of orange smoke came from his mouth.

He seemed to see James and draw courage from him. He headed straight for the roof of James's house. One desperate forepaw grabbed for the television aerial, the other snatched at the chimney-pot. With a terrible tearing sound, the TV aerial was ripped loose and the chimney-pot wobbled. Lassie balanced for a brief second on the very top of the roof and then they heard the eerie unknown call of a dragon wailing in distress as he slid down the roof on the far side. Then they heard an awful crash as he smashed into the next-door neighbour's garden shed.

James and his dad tore round into the back garden. It looked as if a hurricane had come through it.

The fence between them and next door was squashed flat. The little shed where Mr

Perkins next door kept his lawnmower was smashed to pieces. Slates were trickling off the roof and dropping into the garden like falling rain. Amid all the chaos and confusion was Lassie, looking half-ashamed and half-proud. After all, it *was* his first ever landing. And he was only a very young dragon.

"Lassie!" James shrieked and rushed at him.

Lassie's huge snouty head – he really had grown a lot – turned towards James and the dragon rubbed his head hard against the boy's skinny chest.

"Oh, Lassie!" James said, half-laughing and half-crying. "I'm so glad to see you! I'm so glad you came back! I thought I'd lost you! I thought you'd gone!"

Lassie's big scaly arms came clumsily around James and held him close. It was like being hugged by a grizzly bear wrapped in tin foil, but James was so pleased to get his pet back that he didn't mind at all. He put his arms as far as he could reach around Lassie's trunk-like neck and hugged him back.

"Very touching, I'm sure," said a sharp, horrid voice. It was beastly Mr Perkins from next door. "But who's going to pay for my garden shed? Who's going to pay for my tomatoes? Who's going to pay for my time and trouble in growing them to have them squashed flat by that thing? And who's going to promise that it will be gone by tomorrow morning or I'm calling the police?"

James clutched Lassie even tighter.

"He can't go!" he said. "He's my pet. He's my . . . he's my . . . he's my greyhound puppy."

It sounded silly even to James. Greyhounds, however fast and intelligent, do not soar over rooftops and crash-land on other people's greenhouses.

Mr Perkins looked sour. "Greyhound rubbish!" he said. "I'll have the law on you! I want full compensation and that animal gone by tomorrow or I'll call the police."

He stamped into his house and slammed the door so hard that another tile slid slowly off his roof and fell with a tinkle on top of the others.

Dad said nothing. James said nothing. Lassie gave a deep, hot sigh.

The back door opened and James's mam came out.

"Come on in, you three," she said kindly. "We'll think of something. Something'll come up. Something usually does."

James's dad shook his head. He looked frightened. James had never seen his dad look afraid before. But the cost of the garden shed alone was more than they had in their savings, and there was the roof to repair as well. All of their joy at the amazing triumphant return of Lassie the little pet

dragon had disappeared. It was like a night-mare in which everything had suddenly gone wrong.

"It's a shame about the shed," said Christine from the garden on the other side.

Her twins leaned over the garden fence and nodded in agreement. "And after your wonderful dragon came back home like that!"

"We'll work it out. We'll find the money,"
James's mam said as they went indoors. But
she didn't say where they would find it.
"We'll borrow it, if we have to." But they
didn't know anyone who had money to lend.
"I'll do an extra shift cleaning, I'll work
Sundays." But they all knew that there were
no extra shifts which she could work, and
even if there had been, office cleaners are
never paid very much. Certainly not enough
for a new garden shed and new tiles for the
roof.

"It's got me beat," Dad said. His voice was tired and sad. He sounded like a man who had run out of hope. James saw him look towards the cold, empty steel mill, the wide mouths of the chimneys gaping at the sky. No one made steel any more in their town.

It was a sad, quiet tea. Lassie tried not to be in the way, coiling himself up tight and holding his breath so as not to let the smoke out. But it was obvious that he was too big for the kitchen.

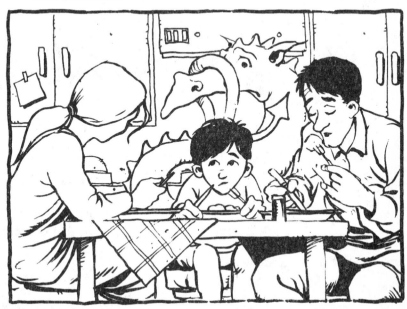

"He'll have to go, James," his mam said sadly. "I'm sorry, but the house just isn't big enough for us all. And if Mr Perkins wants to be nasty about it he could call the police."

James could feel his chin wobbling and hot, sharp tears stinging behind his eyelids.

"But where can he go, Mam?" he asked in a very small voice.

"We'll try the zoo," Dad said. "Or maybe a wildlife park. Somewhere he could be free. But your mam's right, James – he can't stay with us any more."

James hugged Lassie very tight and went out to the garden. There were a few sweet-smelling wallflowers which had not been squashed when Lassie crash-landed. James picked them for Lassie and brought them in to him.

"If only you could make a living from your gardening, his mam said to his dad. "You grow such lovely flowers on the allotment. And there's that old greenhouse just sitting there."

James's dad shrugged. "You need money to earn money," he said. "I can't afford to buy seeds, and a big greenhouse like that would cost a fortune to heat. There's nothing in the world I'd rather do than grow orchids and send them up the road to sell in Newcastle. But it can't be done. It's not for us."

James's mam nodded. James hugged Lassie again and went slowly up the stairs. He felt so miserable that he even cleaned his teeth properly and put out his light at once, without reading by the light of his torch under the bedcovers. It was worse than losing Lassie the first time, if they had to give him away when he had chosen to come home to them. James snuffled a little in sorrow, and fell asleep.

Chapter 5

"Nothing is ever as bad as you expect it to be."

Grown-ups often say that to children to cheer them up when they are dreading something. Sometimes it is true and something is *not* as bad as you thought it would be. On the other hand . . . sometimes it is a good deal worse. It was worse than James could ever have dreamed when he woke in the morning. His mam and his dad were looking serious and the kitchen was looking empty.

"Lassie's gone," his dad said. "Your mam opened the door to let him out into the garden for his morning run and he made a great leap into the air and flew off."

James blinked stupidly. "But he's only just learned to fly," he said. "Just yesterday. He had to run at top speed to take off then. He couldn't just jump up and fly."

"He did though," his mam said. "Straight up, like a big fat butterfly." Her voice shook a little. "I'm sorry," she said. "I didn't think he'd fly off when he'd just come back to us. I'm sorry, James."

"S'all right," James said. Although it wasn't.

James's mam turned her back on James and clattered the mugs as she made tea. James ate his breakfast as if every mouthful was blotting paper.

"D'you think he knew what we were saying?" he asked after a long while. "When you were saying that we couldn't keep him? D'you think he knew we didn't want him? D'you think we hurt his feelings?"

James's mam shook her head. "If he was clever enough to understand what we were saying, then he'd have been clever enough to know we wanted to keep him very much," she said. "He knew we loved him. Perhaps he was always a wild dragon, and he's gone back to wherever he came from."

James nodded and pulled on his jacket, said goodbye to his mam and dad and headed for school. He dawdled all the way along the little road, looking up into the sky and staring at the horizon, but Lassie wasn't there.

He didn't think he'd ever see him again.

James spent the day staring hopelessly out of the school window, watching and waiting to see if Lassie would come home. All evening he sat at his bedroom window watching the sun slowly sink over the allotments till its red light made all the panes of the old greenhouse burn like fire. He sat and watched until the moon rose – a big, golden moon which could have lit Lassie's way home to James. He waited and waited, hoping that at any minute he would see the great ungainly silhouette of his dragon pass across in front of the moon, beating his huge wings.

"You'll catch your death of cold," Mam said. She had been out at her cleaning job and she smelled waxy and sweetly of floor polish. She came into James's bedroom and hugged him tight. "Into bed," she said. "There's nothing to see out there."

The way she spoke told James that she too had been looking up into the night sky as she walked home from work, hoping to see Lassie coming home.

All this time Lassie was flying and flying, like a huge determined green seagull, through the day and through the night. He flew across a great grey tumbling ocean and then flew on, even further. He flew through a rainstorm, when the air seemed to thicken all around him and rain pattered noisily against his scales like rain on a corrugated iron roof. Then it grew light again and the sun came up and the air got warmer. Still Lassie flew on, pointing south, his head stretched before him, his wings beating and beating. The sun grew bright and the sea grew dazzling and blue beneath his dangling feet. Hot air currents swelled under his wings, bearing him up. The winds gathered behind his fat bottom and sped him southward, southward, over a sea which was bluer than any sea Lassie had ever seen.

Over a sea as blue as bluebells, over a sea as blue as delphiniums, and then over a sea as blue as violets Lassie flew until he could see ahead of him a dark smudge on the horizon. The sight gave Lassie energy, and he beat his wings harder, flying strongly towards it. It was a secret island, hidden away from everyone, unknown to any map, with jungle as thick as icing on fudge cake coating the top of the island and tumbling down the sides to beaches of white sand.

Lassie was very tired. He put out his broad feet and let himself flop down on to the soft sand. He stretched his front legs forward and his back legs back, laid his great neck and horny head down on the hot sand and fell fast asleep.

When he awoke it was evening, and above him unknown stars hung in the dark sky like huge yellow lamps. Lassie yawned and sat up and looked around. He had landed

near a stream which trickled through the jungle and then spread out on the sand and oozed away into the sea, like a wet fan. Lassie paddled in the stream, soothing his hot feet and scooping up piles of sand into little sandcastles. When he was tired of playing he

started walking inland, following the course of
the stream, wading upstream, pushing his
shoulders against the trees and creepers of the
jungle, going deeper and deeper, pausing now
and then to lap from the water, or to reach up
and eat a fragrant hanging flower.

All around him were the secret sounds of the jungle – a squawk from a dreaming parrot, the stirring of a troupe of monkeys, the chatter of night insects, and the quiet gulps of frogs. Lassie's eyes glowed as bright as marmalade. He was very happy. He was not at all afraid of the dark or the strangeness of the place. He knew he was the biggest animal on the whole island – possibly the biggest

animal in the world. And besides, he was a very sweet-tempered dragon. He did not believe that anyone or anything would hurt him, so he was afraid of nothing. His feet in

cool soothing water, his nose questing for the sweetest flowers, Lassie paddled his way inland, to the very heart of the island.

The stream widened ahead of him to make a deep freshwater pool. Lassie sighed with pleasure, a little curl of smoke rising from his nose, and eased himself deep into the water till it lapped over his shoulders and around his outstretched weary wings. On the edge of the pool there was a little hut. Lassie wallowed in the cool stream and soft sandy mud like a great fat green lady in a bubble bath, and watched the door of the hut as it slowly opened.

An old man came out. He wore a gown of
deep midnight blue marked with moons and
stars and rolling suns and burning comets. In
the dark of the jungle the embroidery of his
gown glowed with a silver light like a hundred
little torches to light his way. On his head was
a tall triangular hat. He had a white flowing
beard and long white flowing hair. In one
thin hand he carried a long silver sceptre.

"Artemis!" he said with pleasure when he saw Lassie. "I sensed that you were coming."

Lassie beamed at him and a little wisp of smoke came through his smiling teeth.

"Grown a good deal, I see," the magician said approvingly. "'They must be feeding you well?"

Lassie's eyes were warm at the thought of James, and James's mam and dad.

Meehort the magician nodded. "Dragons *are* expensive to keep," he said. "And little boys even worse. I daresay I should have sent more money for your keep. What shall I do? Send a chest of pirate gold?"

Lassie shook his great head very slowly. Meehort frowned for a moment and then tipped his head on one side as if he were listening.

"Flowers!" he exclaimed. He listened again. "Orchids!" he said. "Well, you've come to the right place for orchids!"

He paused for a few more moments of silence while Lassie stared into his face, nodding his green head and waving his spiny tail in the water.

"Certainly! Certainly!" Meehort said pleasantly. "I'll get you a sack."

He went back into the hut and came out again with a very small paper bag in his hand. Lassie looked at it with his knobbly little eyebrows raised.

Meehort chuckled. "It's bigger than it looks," he said.

Lassie took the little bag in one great green paw.

"Pick Your Own," Meehort said pleasantly. "Help yourself. Eat some flowers before you go, Artemis; it's a long flight home." He patted Lassie's scaly neck and then turned and went towards his little hut.

"Come again," he said. "Any time. My gosh, you *have* shot up, haven't you? And out. And along."

He waved kindly to Lassie and went into
his hut and shut the door. A bubble of smoke,
pink and shining, floated out of the chimney

and hung in the air, lighting up the jungle all around. Holding the paper bag carefully in his scaly paw, Lassie heaved himself out of the water and waddled over to the trees.

It is not easy collecting the seeds of rare and valuable orchids when you have two large paws each with three golden knife-like claws, and only a very small paper bag to put the seeds in. The young dragon knew that

seeds should always be left on the plant to make new plants. But this was a magic island and the seeds and roots grew again the moment Lassie gathered them.

The bag looked no bigger from the outside, but somehow there was always room for another seed or root. It was a fiddly and difficult task for a young dragon. In the end he found the easiest method was to nip off the seed-heads with his mouth and spit the seeds carefully into the paper bag.

He sat back on his plump tail and sucked and spat – just like you might eat cherries and spit the stones – for a long, long time, until the stars faded and the great orange tropical moon went down behind the darkness of the jungle trees. Even then, Lassie carried on collecting his seeds, and carefully, very carefully, digging and cutting roots lit by the shining pink bubble of smoke which hung above Meehort's hut.

When the morning sun came up in a rush of yellow heat Lassie had finished. In his hand he had a bag filled with orchid seeds and orchid roots. It was a wonderful collection – more rare flowers than anyone had ever collected before. He paddled back down the

river, nibbling at flowers as he went, and then he sat for a little while on the golden beach, watching the turquoise waves rolling in and washing against the shore.

When he was rested, the young dragon took his paper bag firmly in one paw, and flung himself in a great gallop along the sandy beach, beating his wings and straining to leap upwards. With a few great strides he made it!

The warm currents of air from the island lifted him upwards and he circled around looking down. Below him was the stream and Meehort's hut, and Meehort's pink smoke bubble. Lassie waved a paw to the hut and the smoke bubble waved back and popped. Lassie turned his head for the north, stretched out his body in the warm air, and beat his wings steadily and strongly, heading for James and home.

Chapter 6

James was rounding the corner into his street, trailing his school bag behind him, when the sun was suddenly blocked, and a great shadow fell on him and then passed down the street.

James looked up into the sky and let out a shriek which had his mam and dad tumbling out of their front door to see what was the matter. There, in the sky above the street, at roof-top height, Lassie was circling, trying to land. He had the knack of it now. He lined himself up with the road like a jumbo jet lines up with a runway. He flew slower and slower, sank down to about two metres off the ground and then dropped like a small avalanche. The street rocked slightly, but nothing was actually broken.

James pelted forward and flung his arms around Lassie's great neck.

"Lassie!" James's mam called, and she ran outside with a handful of rose petals to welcome him home.

Lassie carefully laid the paper bag at their feet and beamed at them.

"What's this?" James asked. He opened the bag and looked inside. "It's only seeds," he said, disappointed. "And roots and things. Why did you bring us these, Lassie?"

James's dad took the bag and looked in. James could see his face changing. First he looked surprised, then he looked amazed, and then his face crumpled as if he might laugh aloud or cry. "Seeds," he said, "and fresh roots! Orchid seeds and roots!"

He looked at Lassie. "Where have you been?" he asked. "Where did you get them? This is the most amazing collection I have ever seen in my life!"

Lassie's eyes beamed a bright ruby colour. He did not say anything. He could not say anything.

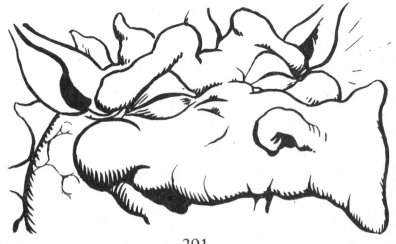

"Did you bring them for us?" Mam asked. Lassie puffed a curl of delighted golden smoke in reply.

"I could make my fortune with these," James's dad said. "They're fresh, they're ready for planting. They're an amazing collection. I could plant them, and grow them! I could . . . I could . . ."

James put his arm over his dragon's neck and watched his dad. His dad looked somehow different. He looked taller, he looked younger. He was pink with excitement and stammering.

"We could plant them in pots and keep them in the house," he said. "If we turned the whole of the upstairs into a greenhouse . . . I suppose we could grow them . . ."

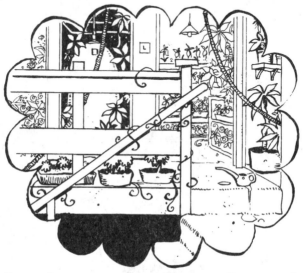

James's mam was smiling at James's dad with love in her eyes. "We can't plant them in the house, pet," she said gently. "There isn't room."

"Then I'll build a greenhouse!" James's dad said determinedly. "This is the chance of a lifetime for us and we are going to take it.

Lassie has brought us a miracle. An absolute miracle! Somewhere, somehow I'm going to get a greenhouse and make these flowers grow!"

Lassie leaned forward and gave James a poke in the shoulder with his bony nose. James turned around. Lassie was beaming at him, his eyes bright. A little curl of smoke came from each nostril.

"What?" James asked.

Lassie's rosy eyes implored James to think. He puffed a tiny cloud of smoke into James's face and James stepped back from the heat.

"What?" James said again. Then he yelled, "Of course! I see! It's brilliant! You're a genius! A genius, Lassie!"

He grabbed hold of his mam's hand and his
dad's arm. His dad kept tight hold of the bag
of plants and Lassie galloped before them as
James towed his mam and dad down the
garden path, through the back garden,
through the little gate into their allotment,
and across all the allotments to the old
greenhouse which stood empty and cold in
the corner of the site.

The door hung open and a few panes of glass were broken. The boiler was rusty and damp in the corner. James darted towards it and flung open the boiler door. It was filled with old wet coke stuck together in a hopeless cold lump. It had been years and years since the boiler had been lit – years and years since the greenhouse had been warm.

"Go on!" James yelled, jumping up and down in delight. "Go on!"

James's mam and dad looked at each other in amazement, but Lassie and James understood each other. Lassie bent his great snouty head towards the open door of the boiler, and with a beaming smile as broad as a crocodile's grin he blew a deep, burning blast of breath into the very heart of the boiler.

At once it caught light and began to warm up. The coke glowed bright as a furnace. Little whispers of steam came from vents in the walls. The greenhouse windows, all thickly misted with the damp of many years, started to steam and clear. The pipes all around the greenhouse clicked as they warmed. Somewhere a tap dripped – a lush, wet springlike sound.

"Yes!" James's dad cried out. "Yes! This would do for my plants all right!"

"And Will Groves's tomatoes," James's mam said.

"And everybody's early seedlings," James's dad added excitedly. "It's such a huge greenhouse and it belongs to the allotments – everyone should use it. We could all repair it, we could help each other. If Lassie would heat it for us . . ." he hesitated. "*Would* you heat it for us, Lassie?"

Lassie's eyes glowed as bright as the coals. He nodded delightedly. Then he rolled his head towards James like a cat wanting a stroke.

James flung his arms around his pet's hot, scaly neck.

"Was there ever a dog like this?" he demanded.

James's mam and dad called a meeting of everyone in the street, and all of them (even miserable Mr Perkins next door) agreed that they would get together and rebuild the greenhouse, and together grow flowers, vegetables and plants.

James's mam gave up her cleaning job and worked in the greenhouse with James's dad and the other neighbours. She stopped smelling of cleaning polish and her face grew brown and sunny instead of white and tired. In the first year they made enough money to pay everyone a proper wage, and in the second year they made a small profit. In a little while the allotments and greenhouse became quite famous and they called themselves Dragon Plants in honour of Lassie.

They always have the earliest flowering plants of any garden centre, because they keep their greenhouse so hot. Even in midwinter you can buy roses and strawberries from the Dragon Plants shop. Even at

Christmas you can buy fresh rare flowers. The beautiful rich ladies of Yorkshire and Durham send to Dragon Plants for orchids to pin to their evening dresses, and flowers to perfume their rooms. Sometimes they come to the shop and walk around the greenhouses. They give James's dad enormous orders for plants and pay with huge cheques.

Sometimes they pat James on the head and call him "perfectly sweet", and he has learned to smile and not make sick noises.

Sometimes things go wrong in the greenhouse. They have had their failures. Once they lost a whole tray of seedlings because they got too hot and dry, and one lady complained that her roses were scorched, as if they had been near smoke – but that was obviously impossible. They told her that they could not imagine how the petals had got so hot and crumpled, and they gave her a fresh bouquet.

James has a little sister now, and when his mam is working in the greenhouse she often puts the pram out in the garden. She is a happy baby and never cries, for there is always

someone to rock her to sleep. Someone once said they thought they saw a large green tail tipping the pram gently to and fro. But that is obviously impossible too. It must have been an odd trick of the light.

James still does not have a bike, although he is now eleven. But he does not mind at all. Who wants to cycle when you and all your friends can climb on to the great green back of your very own dragon, and fly higher and higher in the sky, all the way to the South Seas, where the water turns as blue as bluebells, as blue as delphiniums, and then as blue as violets, and there is a secret island, unknown to any map, and a wizard called Meehort who always has your favourite tea ready and waiting for you?